Rescue Pup

A special dog,
a big adventure,
a happy ending!

Written by
Brenda Fiorini

Illustrations by
Nathan Behmlander

MW01041812

This book is dedicated to all those who rescue animals
--B.F.

To Karen Bernardo, editor, and John Reinhardt, book designer for all your
encouragement and expert knowledge in helping to create this story and book design.

In memory of Mark Knie, President of Granny Rose Animal Shelter,
for dedicating his lifetime to helping homeless animals.

CHILDREN: Please do not approach a stray, unknown, or wild animal. If you see an animal
that appears wild, homeless or in distress, tell an adult or contact an authority who can help.
Remember, safety first!

Granny Rose Animal Shelter
613 River Lane, Dixon, Illinois, 61021

A nonprofit 501(c)(3) organization whose mission is to promote the humane care and treatment of all animals in Lee, Ogle and Whiteside counties of Illinois. Our shelter survives strictly from donations and fundraisers. We provide a warm and loving environment, proper care, and spay/neuter services for every cat and dog that becomes a resident of our shelter. We work diligently to find loving homes for the abandoned and homeless animals within our area, and to foster humane education, including proper care and the benefits of spay/neuter through our **Read! Write! Rescue!** program.

Complete classroom kits are available upon request.
Please contact us for more information.
grannyroseanimalshelter@hotmail.com
www.grannyrose.org
815-288-PETS (7387)

613 River Lane, Dixon, IL 61021

Every year millions of animals are abandoned for various reasons and find their way to shelters and rescues where they await a second chance to find a loving home. There are many happy, loveable and loyal cats and dogs that are looking for a family who can return the same kindness.

What you can do:

Contact or visit a local animal shelter to learn more.
Ask questions about adoption procedures.
Research and learn about responsible pet care.
Research the breed characteristics of your potential adoptee.
Contact a local veterinarian to find out about pet care costs.
Spay/neuter your pet

On the far edge of town
in the thick of the woods
curved a long winding road
where a tiny house stood.

All alone in that house sat a pup who was sad.
There was no one to play with—
no friends to be had.

While he waited
and watched
for the door
to unlock,
it grew dark
in the house.

Then he heard
a loud knock!

There was no one outside, just the wicked old winds
that ripped through the trees and tore down the limbs!
As dark gloomy clouds blew over the moon,
lightning bolts flashed and thunder ka-BOOMED!

The little dog dashed up the stairs, down the hall,
and he shook all night long
from the sounds of the squall.

By morning the storm
was over and done.
The rain cleared up
and out came the sun.

The puppy was hungry.
He looked all around
for water and food—

there was none
to be found!

Soon day became night
and then
daytime once more,
but no one came home
to unlock the front door.

So he howled
and he whimpered
in terrible fear,
that no one
would rescue him—
no one would hear!

This poor lonesome pup couldn't wait any more,
so he clawed at the windows and pawed on the doors.
He pushed on a screen—scratched a hole 'til it grew.
Then he twisted and shoved,
and squeezed his way through.

He was free now at last
as he crept very slow...

through the woods
and the darkness,
not sure where to go.

Coming out of the trees,
he found danger too soon.

He was chased down the path
by a mean old raccoon.

As he ran through a field
there were sharp prickly burrs
that stuck to his toes and his legs and his fur.

He was hurt once again on his way into town
when he stepped on some glass
that was scattered around.

He kept looking
for someone,
a friend who might care,

but instead
he heard "Scram!"
So he ran!
He was scared!

17

Then he faced the worst danger
of all on that night –
A highway! Fast cars!
Headlights blinding his sight!

He stopped, then he turned,
then he started to go –
When a car blared its horn,
tires screeched, and – OH, NO!

The car quickly stopped; someone opened the door.
The pup froze. Could he possibly take any more?
Then a woman stepped out. "Little Buddy!" she cried.
"Are you lost? Are you hurt? Let me get you inside!"

He was glad to be rescued and happy to find
a friend who could help him – someone who was kind!
The little pup loved his first ride in a car
till the woman said "Buddy, get up! Here we are!"

He followed her into a wonderful place
where he ate and he slept in his own little space.

Many days passed him by.
Many strangers did too.
Would he find a new home?
Would it ever come true?

Then Meg came to visit the shelter one day,
and she noticed this pup in his cage right away.

"Hello, Buddy!" she said with a big shining smile.
"I've wanted a dog for a very long while!"

As he looked up at Meg with his eyes gleaming bright,
Buddy thought to himself,
"She's the one. She's just right!"

When she opened the cage
he jumped into her arms.

Buddy gave her
a lick, and he
poured on the
charm!

"Oh, please! Mom and Dad,
can we take Buddy home?
He's the one. He is special!
I'll make him my own!"

They said, "Meg, you must promise
before we agree
that you'll take care of Buddy
quite seriously!"

"I promise! I'll feed him and walk him each day.
I'll teach him to sit and to come and to stay!

I'll talk to him, pet him,
and love him, you'll see!

I'll be there for him, and he'll be there for me."

So Buddy went home
with his new special friend,

delighted that life
turned out fine in . . .
THE END!